TWISTED OBSESSION

A RIPPTON U DARK HITMAN/STALKER ROMANCE

SOFIA AVES

First Edition

Published by Little Quail Press

Editing by Partners in Crime

EBOOK ISBN 978-1-922448-65-1

PAPERBACK ISBN 978-1-922448-84-2

AUTHOR'S NOTE

TWISTED OBSESSION is a dark romance, and may not be suitable for all readers. If you're coming from my alpha male books where heroes are protectors, please be aware this story takes anti-heroes to a new level. This book is not the same as my other works.

Content warnings include explicit scenes and language, blood play, death, abuse, voyeurism, hostage situations, violence and some unvoiced consent situations.

If the above list doesn't bother you, welcome to my creepy, fucked up mind. It gets lonely occasionally, so, come on in.

Don't forget to lock the door behind you.

the darkness beckons

CHAPTER 1

DANTE

*C*eleste Flores. *My target.*

I watched her through the scope of my rifle where she sat perched on the narrow ledge of her shitty apartment where a supposed kingpin's daughter should never live. Her pale visage glowed like a sacrifice under the moon's darkened hue.

Cold air kissed her skin as it did mine, a shared experience, though she didn't know I watched her as I had for weeks, my obsession building.

She's just a job.

I was simply doing my homework.

On the top of a building, with a scope, and a loaded rifle.

And a named mark.

But my eyes were drawn to her in a magnetic way, like she linked to me somehow. And so tonight, like many other nights, I wouldn't pull the trigger. *Not yet.* Instead, I devoured her with my sight alone.

Fine-boned hands curled around a precariously tilted glass of red wine eking up its bowl. A slim wrist, a toned arm. Hair like moonbeams flicked around her face as the night air lifted the translucent strands as she looked out over the night cityscape. Her expression tasted of melancholy and the bitter seeds of her ennui spread across the hundred yards from my rooftop hideout to her small window.

Gravel dug into my belly through my tactical wear, brutal shards of shattered glass and grit and gravel, though I relished the pain. A short breath rather than a hollow one and my finger feathered the air above the trigger, a shot I had taken a thousand times before.

But as every other night this month, watching her.. something stopped me.

She's just a job.

Perhaps it was the carolers beneath, wending their way across the city, or the gritter of cheap tinsel wound between streetlamps, their banners proclaiming a season of peace.

Perhaps there is no season of peace.

I could keep telling myself that lie, but it wouldn't stick any more than it had for the last three weeks.

Get your shit together, Beaufort.

Her father, kingpin of the outlying city limits, gave me a job. A simple one.

Get rid of an asset.

Easy, right?

An asset, a deadly one...who happened to be his daughter.

Fucking delightful.

Fucking family actually, by my standards. I left mine alone a long time back, walking from the bodies of my mother and father and their crew who planned to gang rape a girl tied to the table with tinsel where we ate every night.

That sort of experience tended to ruin Christmas.

Shifting on my spot, I lost her for a moment, then swore, berating myself for both speaking and for letting my tarnished memories fuck with my focus as I readjusted my scope.

Her window—when I finally found it, the wind picked up slightly, and I made another adjustment—that window I had become obsessed with was empty.

What the actual fuck?

I watched her for the last weeks while her father griped at me about not getting the job done. She always had the same routine. It never varied. Predictability made for easy prey, but it also made for pretty watching with an innocent girl who sat in that window, staring out at the city like she floated above it. Or perhaps she should be beneath it with me, walking in the darkest of shadows, where light couldn't penetrate.

But she was always in that window, starlight illuminating her face, her never drunk wine glass dangling listless in her hand. The window where nothing on the other side stopped her from falling if she did. A single misstep, a hard wind or a gentle push, and her life would spread over the filthy alley below, without even a fire escape to break her imminent plummet.

When I finally took the shot, at some future date, would she fall into the darkness of the room beyond her, or slam into the unforgiving grit and filth beneath, soiling her perfect white nightdress, tarnishing her pale hair?

Those were all my worries, my concerns over the kill I should have ended so long ago.

Now, she was gone.

I cursed, swinging the scope down to search the alley, wondering if I would see her body splattered across the stinking urine stains like so much discarded trash. The alley was empty, and a fraction of air sucked into my chest.

If Celeste Flores was to die, it would be by my hand, and mine alone.

Swinging the scope back to my mark's usual spot, her window came into focus in time to register the silver flash coming my way in an impossible arc. A moment held between us, the sweeping movement of her arm, the dull glint of starlight on metal.

I exhaled, and the blade buried itself cement inches from my knees. I stared at it for a second before I laughed.

All those smooth lines, the sharp angles. No, not a blade; an arrow.

She shot at me with a fucking crossbow, missing only by design.

What the actual fuck?

A broad grin spread across my face as I yanked the offending object from its berth, twirling the short length in my fingers. The bolt was rough on one side where several letters were engraved into the polished metal where it rested against my callouses.

I stared at the slightly uneven words she carved in by hand.

I can see you.

That she gave me a capital S earned a soft laugh. She shot at me and missed, but not by error. I smiled, something cracking in my chest, my heart beating in its black blood that filled my veins, and focused on her once more.

She was back in the window as though nothing happened, one leg swinging from its safe haven outside of the window. Her foot was bare and, for some reason, even with the view of her perfectly toned calf wrapped in a white skirt, the sight was erotic. I reached beneath myself to adjust my cock, wishing it was her tender flesh that squeezed the rock hard length.

As I watched, she stared across the hundred yards across the city lights, ignoring the scurrying, inconsequential town beneath us. The many lives we avoided continued in their pathetic chores while we occupied the shadows in the void above. Her eyes connected with mine, jolting me through the magnified vision of the scope.

The faintest smile on her lips, she raised the wineglass she never drank from, taking a single sip. Her head tilted to one side, she lifted the crossbow outside the windowsill, dangling the metal for a brief moment, and let it fall.

Its inaudible clang still reverberated through me as I counted out the seconds to impact, never taking my eyes off her. Not again. With that shot at me, my fascination with her twisted like a macabre obsession, knowing that by ending her life, I would ache for her. A form of possessiveness infested my dark heart like a disease, ruining me more than I already was from the inside out.

I let out a breath, my chest hollow, and feathers the trigger.

Just once.

Glass sprayed in a beautiful array of glittering shards across her lips, exploding the remnants of her red wine into the air like so much bloody rain suspended in the black night's muted light for a frozen moment before they fell, leaving her holding the delicate remains of the jagged glass stem in her lithe fingers.

The impact tossed shards of glass her way, some small pieces embedding around her throat in the creamy expanse of her delicate skin, the trailing drops of blood ghostly against a pale background. One larger drop trailed slowly between her breasts, painting the swell in glistening carmine.

Otherwise she remained unharmed, though her pulse fluttered at the sweet slope of her exposed throat.

Through it all she never took her eyes off me, and she never moved.

Celeste held out the remainder of her glass into the void of nothingness and opened fingers. The glass glittered, flashing in the reflected city lights as it fell, but neither of us were watching it. Perfect soft pink lips parted as she gazed at me, unseeing but piercing through me, and mouthed a single word.

Tomorrow.

My breath lodged in my throat, I kept my scope on her. She reached between her breasts, picking out each slice of glass I put there, marking her one by one, and dropping them over her windowsill. Celeste sent me a final sweet look and slipped from the windowsill here.

My wintergreen, like the star-shaped arctic flower. Delicate, but sharp.

Fucking perfection.

I blinked, but she didn't return to the window, still lying there on my stomach, exposed and made, though she had been gone for more than a minute.

I hadn't killed her. Again.

The shot I hadn't taken should have haunted me, but didn't.

For the first time in my life, I didn't do the job I'd been paid to complete. My hands were busy dismantling my weapon, closing the clasps to its case and rolling to my feet. I brushed glass from my front, one fingertip slicing across a piece of broken bottle, a single drop of blood swelling at the end of the extremity. The drop grew heavy at the bottom end, and just before it fell, I held my hand over the city below.

An offering, a sacrifice.

Like hers.

Her window sat empty no matter how long I waited, and I knew tonight was only the beginning of a force I couldn't halt, couldn't prevent, only ride to its completion. A fresh obsession that would end as it did, an observer in my own fate, drawn inexorably to her.

This was a girl I would break for, because she fascinated me.

She could have killed me, given the chance, but instead she teased me, winding me toward her.

I couldn't do anything less to repay the favor.

A hard smile crossed my face as I took one last glance at her window. This silly season would be fun. I'd hold out on her fate for as long as possible before I ended it on my own terms and no one else's.

Her death was mine.

Whistling a broken carol to match the mangled warble echoing across the city, I strode across the rooftop in full view of my little nemesis.

Yes, we would have fun. I'd unwrap her like the present she was always made to be, one just for me.

My beautiful, twisted obsession.

Merry fucking Christmas to me.

CHAPTER 2

CELESTE

I swept my fingers across the gray squares as they deteriorated across my cement canvas, devolving into deformed diamonds. Under my design, the ground appeared to ripple beneath my feet as I crossed the studio room my professor gave me as a space to create my major project for the year.

Not that Rippton U, with all its wealth and egos, didn't have a lack of space or vacant rooms. I paid my tithe to the college directly from my own funds, but I knew my father injected income into the dean's personal account to ensure what he wanted was what happened.

And so, like with my apartment and its security men stationed outside the door as they did outside my studio, I was imprisoned. A cage of a different color, one of greys enhanced with a rippling spiral in the center drawing the viewer down to a zero point of nothingness that wound internally in its own twisted version of hell.

While other students went home to their families at Christmas, I stayed on campus during my days, working tirelessly at my project in a bid to escape reality. Perhaps that was why I was drawn to optical art.

Perhaps that was why I teased the man sent to kill me.

I even knew who sent him, who expected him to fail.

Being a mafia princess meant my cage defied the rules of men, and my existence was tested daily.

Only if I survived my father's twisted trials would I one day earn the right to his throne.

A throne I'd rather burn, but he set up his life–and belatedly mine also–in a fashion that entwined me to his fate.

If I tried to walk away, I would die.

Playing with death was no easy game but one I

pretended to enjoy when all I wanted was to be ignored, and left to play my own games, disappearing between this reality and the one I created, hiding from the world forever.

I wondered if my new foe was up to the task my father set. Something told me he might be.

Even now, I felt his eyes on me, though it should be impossible in the windowless room.

Perhaps I should paint the walls as well. The door.

Make it an inescapable hell of boxes and spirals, one that sent the viewer mad in an attempt to remove themselves from the type of cage I created.

Perhaps I should put my father in such a room and observe his madness.

There was a slice of stalker in each of us; some was simply harder to unearth than in others.

Like my killer.

A strange relationship blossomed between us where he watched me, and I watched him back, waiting for the brief pain that told me he finally took the shot he'd been paid to do.

Night after night he refused, observing me still and taking no action.

My father wouldn't stand for the lack of satisfaction from either of us in our odd little impasse.

Last week he changed those rules, taking the shot that told him I was no easy target, even if, just once, I wanted to be one.

Let him take the shot, and experience death.

But that would let my father win.

Living allowed my father to win.

And so I made my twists and twirls on the cement flooring, working my way along the bared, striped plaster walls.

Here, no one could touch me in my pretty cage of illusions. My silence remained until my guard knocked harshly on the door I covered in an endless swarm of illusions that defied reality depending on which angle you stared at it from.

Stare too long and...

I smiled, my madness not quite slipping free, and opened the door.

My father's guard took one look at the door and baulked. "Unnatural bitch," he hissed, shoving his gun between my shoulder blades and forcing me out of the room.

"You don't like my gifts," I said sweetly. "What if I was your boss? Would you follow my commands?"

He sneered at me. "You're more damaged than your fucking father. Stupid slut."

I smiled and began to count in my head.

After all, there was no point in alarming the asshole of his imminent demise.

Five, six, seven–

The guard at my back fell to the ground.

I didn't need to check his body to know a perfectly round hole would be pierced through his temple straight to the other side. An odd angle, but a recognizable one. The last four guards each wore a hole like it.

The first I studied, tracing the edges with my fingertip, painting the whirls there a shade of tainted red.

The next day a part of my illusions within my studio also seeped red throughout one corner. I left the color on the grayscale as a reminder of what was hidden, what was missing from my reality.

Life, or the lack thereof.

I smiled, tilting my head back into the waning winter sun. The campus was mostly bereft of students and the professors knew well enough to leave me to my own devices.

I had my own form of protection, after all. My own guard, though I suspected he saw me as an easy version of his prey.

Keeping my steps light, I walked across campus, knowing his eyes were on me. Somehow, under his obsessive gaze, I knew nothing would touch me. He wouldn't allow it.

And somehow, so wrongly, that branding of possession...it felt safe.

The facade of security lasted until nightfall. Until I sat in my window at eleven o'clock, watching the stars flicker above muted city lights, haunting strains of Christmas carols filtering across the open spaces, the star twinkling its fake lights in the neon tree set in the central plaza. Late shoppers wandered freely with only a few nights until the event was over, and the town returned to a muted semblance of itself.

Until I realized that he wasn't there on his rooftop, where he was supposed to be. The man sent to kill me.

Predictability was both a comfort and a curse.

Twirling a fresh wine glass in my fingers, filled with black vodka this time, I searched the nightscape for his familiar form, but there was nothing there. No one.

The city was empty of my stalker.

Fear gripped my stomach. Somewhere along the

last month I taught myself to rely on the regularity of this man and tonight...was different.

I spun the glass in my fingers, allowing the disgusting liquid to slosh across my chest, staining the white silk nightie with its spaghetti straps I replaced the night he shot the glass I held. Small scars decorated my otherwise unblemished skin like a necklace, marking me with his present of the season.

My heart pounded in my chest as I tried to regulate my breaths. A quick glance across at my door showed dual shadowed feet either side. My guards stood there still, but my stalker was missing.

Where are you?

Why aren't you there?

Was this recompense for disappearing that night? I broke my routine, slipping from the windowsill to slip into the bathroom, cleaning myself and my glass up before one of the guards inquired of the noise.

Guards, a joke in itself.

If he shot me, they would leave me to bleed out on my cheap carpet in the shitty apartment I wasn't allowed to change.

A different sort of prison, one where I wasn't

permitted to hide in illusions of my own creation, and so I hid in his instead.

My stalker.

What's your name?

I speak in our odd relationship, which became a one sided affair. He watched me; I waited, seeking contact when he appeared. But only when he wished. He killed for me, but I couldn't find his hiding spot.

The first three times, I tried.

Then I stopped.

Perhaps he wanted me to find him.

I searched the rooftops again, then the windows below. Like that night I held out the glass, tipping its contents to the alley below, letting the dark blood splay into the filth already there, then dropped the glass. When it shattered, I slipped from the window without another look and headed for my bed without washing off the sticky alcohol that burned my skin slightly, an illusion of its own, the sins from within escaping to consume the layer of flimsy material I wore.

Black hadn't been his choice, it was mine. All the greyscapes, all monochrome where he added a highlight of red to the mix.

My mine was broken by my father's twisted,

fucked up games he played with me since I was a child, a never ending sting of killers, all of them a disappointment, an easy target, until this one.

I didn't know his name. I didn't understand his game.

Now, he was gone.

And I mourned.

CHAPTER 3

DANTE

Celeste left her window open.

It was a habit born of our form of communication, our game. Like she welcomed me into her night with an open invitation.

Tonight, I took that invitation.

Sliding my legs over her ledge, I paused, watching her where she lay still on her bed, covered in something dark, something that wasn't usually there.

The rules of our game changed.

My heart lurched in its constricting cavity. Though the urge to leap across the room to check her, to feel her pulse flutter under my fingers and ensure her life was still mine to take, I waited, watched. Checked she was alone, and her guards were still outside.

Knowing they were there while I invaded the space her father made for her hardened my cock. Swallowing, I jumped softly onto the industrial carpet that stank of a hundred tenants before her. He father was a pig, either trying to kill his daughter, or torture her, all to make her into the perfect heir for his false kingdom.

She already holds a power you can't comprehend, filthy fucker.

I sneered at the thought of him, knowing tomorrow I'd decline a job which would end in myself being hunted and a death or twenty at some future point. Mine, or someone else's. It didn't really matter.

The room stood empty, apart from us. I crossed the space in a few long strides, standing over her body, and prepared for her death.

Her chest rose beneath the black stain that trickled into the valley between, across the marks I gave her the week before, their pale flesh gleaming against her perfect skin. Not so perfect where I broke her, marked her.

I trailed my fingers through the mess that stained both her skin and nightdress, bringing them to my mouth. The faded sting of alcohol and something bitter dragged across the tip of my tongue.

Vodka, squid's ink, and something else. I rolled the fluid around in my mouth, watching her. *She* had done this to herself, defiled her beautiful body. I leaned forward, letting my saliva drip from my lips, mixed with the foul liquid.

It fell onto her chest in a small pool as I repeated the process. When there was enough, I traced my fingers across the mixture, washing her with my fluids. Her skin was soft and yielded gently under my touch, dressing perfectly. I nearly came in my pants like a boy with his first five dollar whore.

But she was priceless. My Wintergreen.

Her breaths shuddered and she let out a sigh in her sleep, her shoulders rolling, disturbed from my touch.

I smiled into the darkness, freeing my cock in one hand, tracing my saliva lightly over her silk covered nipples with the other. Her flesh beaded into hard points, and the next sigh that slipped from her lips was more a moan than anything else.

My erection ached in my hand, steel hard and I knew I could come without touching myself while I violated her. That was the twisted power she held over me, the inability to kill her, the obsession to *possess* her, own her body, her mind...

Resting one knee lightly on the bed, I leaned forward, brushing the head of my cock across her lips while I played with her restless body. She twitched beneath my touch, her legs spreading slightly, her fingers stroking the sheets at her side.

Those breasts, her heavy, perfect globes would fit well in my palms but for tonight the tiniest touches left us both aching, craving. Should I leave her satisfied or needy? My lust should mirror hers, whatever the outcome of tonight. I smiled at that; perhaps I could give her what her tarnished little body needed.

Trapping her nipples lightly between my knuckles and tugging, I played with her body, learning the things she liked as her pulse fluttered weakly at her throat in the dim, reflected city lights in this room, barren of life.

Not like the art she created.

I'd been in her studio, defiled that with my own markings, though I knew she was yet to discover them, writing my name inside one of the endless coils she painted, locked in her own hell.

Now, she was locked in mine.

I squeezed the tip of her nipple enough to give

her the briefest jolt of pain. Her body shuddered, her cry beautiful as her lips opened and I plugged the moans of her impending orgasm with the head of my cock.

She convulsed around me, sucking automatically, like the beautiful creature she was. Her guard today called her bitch and slut—neither words I'd allow on this bewitching creature. So fucking exquisite. I ended his life, her father's stupid version of security, taking his soul for my own collection, and now I would steal hers as well.

Celeste licked and sucked on me, her lips parting enough in her sleep to warn me of her waking, and her of my presence.

Swearing softly, I pulled my swollen cock from her lips with a sweet little *pop*, and decorated her scars with fresh pearls of my cum. Her eyes flickered, and she gasped, one hand reaching between her legs. Her fingers came away wet. I stared at the glistening digits for a second before common sense told me to run.

That didn't stop my body from doing what was needed, and my cock was hard before I reached her window.

Before she opened her eyes, I was gone, wishing I'd tasted her cum for myself, though I'd given her the gift of mine. For now, that would be enough. But soon I would want more.

And I'd take it from her, knowing that beautiful creature was mine to play with, her body already reacting to my taste, my touch, even if her mind did not.

A small smile twisted my lips. I'd never played the game like this before but fuck me if I didn't enjoy breaking her to know me, crave me, even in her dreams.

"You are supposed to be one of the best." Mandillion Flores, Celeste's father and the man who wanted his own offspring slaughtered as fast as possible, sneered in my ear.

Meant to be...one of...

I smiled at the receiver. Once, I would have cared about those caveats, those barbs. Once, my pride might have gotten in my way.

That was many stolen souls ago.

Now, I don't care.

My obsession took precedence.

"I returned your money." Those were the only

words I spoke, softly, not rising to his intended slight.

"Fuck you. I thought you could do the job. Now you know my intent, you'll be on your own hit list." Not passing to address a single issue I raised, he laughed, and I imagined if I stood in front of him he might have levelled a gun in my face, this obtuse man of emerald cloth, or of Oz.

"Good luck." I went to end the call.

"Wit–" Mandillion coughed, as though panicked.

You should be, pretend mafia man.

He didn't hold half the power he made out to possess, but then, most of them didn't. Without their support crew of killers and blood runners, none of these men were. Some of the women were far more corrupt, and much better at taking that power and wielding it.

I wondered what Celeste would do if I killed her father instead of her. Would she rise, too? Or slink away into the shadows, the ones she stared at nightly?

Tonight would be different. Our silent conversation would have words, and touches. Perhaps. Or perhaps I'd slide into her room, meld with the shadows and violate her space with my presence.

Perhaps I'd return her little arrow. I'd kept it in my pocket, wondering how to best put it to use.

"I'm waiting." The words burned my throat like so much acid.

"I'll double the pay."

"No."

The fast words and faster response stalled him.

"I'll–"

"The offer is no longer available." I said coldly. "If I choose to kill her, it will be on my own terms. Anyone else who comes to harm her will find their eternity dues come early."

Her father spluttered in my ear as I ended the call. I should have cut her father off as soon as he rang. Right now I had a different little morsel to tease, though anticipation was half the battle.

Did she know I was coming for her? Did she expect me to run and hide after her shot at me? I was under no disillusions that she missed; the wide shot was intentional, despite the wind. She'd taken it into consideration and placed the arrow perfectly.

I hadn't stayed to see if she knew it was me who defiled her, or if she slept through my abuse of her perfect body, showering my seed from her skin.

Or maybe she knew, and wore it still, letting me mark her again.

swallowed at that last thought, stroking my

She'd finish at her studio soon, and her guard would be there to leer at her. My bike was the fastest way to her campus from my mountain, its heel tracks easy to hide in the thick forest that grew off to one side. The lack of people made it both easy and difficult to infiltrate the building opposite hers, where I set up my rifle to target her guards.

But only if they were out of line.

I fingered the bolt in my pocket, the one with a message of my own engraved on its dulled surface. She would know I was coming for her, and this time I wouldn't allow her to sleep through my touch.

My bike purred beneath me, a living beast in its own right as I rode across the city to her campus and found my regular spot on the rooftop, an easy shot and easier escape.

This time, I didn't have my rifle, but extracted the crossbow I salvaged from her alleyway from the night she dropped her own.

Celeste flores. Artist, illusionist. Princess, killer.

A dichotomy of innocence and depravity and I would make her mine, just like the word I engraved on the opposite side of the bolt, the one she mouthed at me across the void of shadows that night when she first showed me she knew I was there.

Tonight.

She emerged from the studio, her pale hair flowing behind her, the long gray dress she wore with her boots and a jacket strapping her into the material. Her guard shoved her forward–*would they never learn?*–calling her all the unoriginal names he could muster. That moment, that was when I delivered my message to his temple.

He dropped, and the difference of no audible shot turned her on her heel. Celeste kneeled as she had the first day I killed her guard, tracing her finger around the wound. She extracted the bolt with a firm yank, running her fingers along its length to paint a scarlet path into the word I etched opposite hers.

She nodded, leaving the bolt carefully on the ground and walked away.

A smile bloomed over my face.

This night would be ours, together.

She knew I would come, and maybe she would fight, maybe she wouldn't.

I wasn't sure what I wanted from her more.

CHAPTER 4

CELESTE

I left my door unlocked, though I wasn't sure he would use it. What I was certain of was that my stalker had been in my room the night before, that he touched me. Okay, I was ninety percent certain he was in my room. Or perhaps the invasion only happened in my dreams, and I came from a fantasy that broke me without his presence.

I woke sticky, clammy and dripping this morning, my thighs aching like they strained around a hard fantasy of a body, my breasts heavy, my nipple raw. Perhaps the alcohol did burn me. Perhaps I imagined everything.

Perhaps, perhaps.

But perhaps not.

The sharp scent of oranges and something darker, like chocolate, drifted about my room when I woke, a scent I'd tasted on the edges of my tongue when I walked into my studio after a weekend off not so long ago. And I wondered, then, too.

My dream ended when the fullness in my mouth disappeared, the break in my dream jerking me out of my slumber. I dozed fitfully for the next hours until the sun rose, my fingers between my legs, playing with myself but not letting myself come, until I ached and was fatigued with it.

And when his message told me this strange connection we shared––that I welcomed–would end.

My torture, or his.

Tonight.

And I had a few hours until sunset to prepare.

When the sun sank below the horizon, decorating the small city in a haze between a blanket of darkness and midnight blue studded with emerging stars, I lay in my bed, a clean crossbow bolt in one hand and a knife under my pillow.

The window wasn't an option tonight–too easy

for him to pull me out onto the ground below. I might not fight death off now as hard as I once did, knowing my father would likely win at his fuck up games one day, but I didn't want to splat on an alleyway, to be found by police and shrouded in yellow tape and coroner's clinical gloves.

If he was going to kill me, I'd take the death, but rather than be left abandoned, I wanted him to whisk my body away as he did the guards he killed, leaving nary a spot of blood to mourn their passing.

Some stupid romantic notion I possessed.

Between my father and my obsesser, I remained a broken, twisted thing. The only light I kept in my room this time was a small white Christmas tree that glowed with a pale, uncolored white light in one corner, to celebrate the season's passing.

Possibly one of ours.

Maybe something else.

But I wouldn't make either path easy, nor would I give in to my own desire to let whatever happened just...happen. To relinquish control entirely, by choice for the first time.

Forcing my eyes shut, I listened, trying not to wriggle in my sheets or reach for the knife. My fingers clenched around the bolt in my hand, digging my nails into its deadly ridges. My life or his.

That was tonight's bargain. Wasn't it? I swallowed and tried to settle, but it was too early for sleep to blanket me when I had a habit of not drifting until after midnight most nights, watching the city in its seasonal frenzy.

While he watched me in an intimate, silent conversation that became all encompassing. The only thing that allowed me to forget his nearly constant presence was my art.

Unable to cure my restlessness, I padded to the kitchenette, sucking down too much water and hoping I didn't earn myself a need to pee at the wrong moment before I returned to my bed. Smoothing my soft cotton nightie over my body, I clutched at the bolt as a lifeline, one I could cut his with, should the need arise.

Doubt of *everything* set in as I took a physical inventory of myself for the first time, my father's cage too tight to allow menial things such as boys or dating Art was my only outlet and I didn't see myself as I suspected my father's men would.

My body wasn't feminine, with hardly any curves as I often forgot to eat in the studio. I crossed my ankles, rubbing one foot over the other. Rest had to come. I could meditate, something. Forcing myself still, I painted the insides of my eyelids, creating patterns while I let my mind wander into the depths of the swirls I created.

A massive mistake, the potentially life-ending sort.

Because when a noise that shouldn't be there woke me from my drifting unconsciousness, and he appeared in my window, I knew his game was so much more complex than mine.

I sat up suddenly, and my wrists snared on a limit they shouldn't have. Worse, my hands were empty.

And my stalker, the man as obsessed with me as I had become with him, that man crouched on my windowsill, one arm swaying gently as he leaped into the room, a blade glinting at thigh level.

I couldn't run to him or from him; I couldn't do anything. My hands were tied to a short rope connected to my bed head, separate from each other, a full three feet apart. My mouth opened, but nothing emerged. Not a single sound, though my vocal cords strained to the point of splitting. I choked on my panic as he stalked across the carpet to my bed, closing the short distance between us with sure steps that brought him to my side where I half-arched from my mattress.

The room swam behind him, and my throat

thickened, swelling enough to allow the plaintive sound that managed to emerge while my breath, though thin, managed to fill my lungs.

"You drank the water," he murmured, continuing our one-sided conversation as I mewled pathetically. "Don't worry, they won't hear you." He nodded toward the door where the guard's shadows were noticeably absent in the slim strip of light from the hallway outside. "They won't hear anything anymore."

You killed them. I mouthed the words rather than trying to speak, recognizing he stripped that avenue of communication from me.

He nodded, a smile spreading across arched, almost aristocratic bow-shaped lips. His brow was heavy, but the rest of his features were fair; blond hair swung over his face in jagged edges and a long scar decorated the cheek I could see. His eyes were fathomless pools of obsidian, the hard line of his nose creating an unyielding face that was more than handsome. In all, he was so good looking it was painful.

Everything he wore was black. From the tactical looking jersey strapped with a black holster to the black combat pants and boots on his feet. His body filled the clothing out as though it was painted to his skin.

But his eyes, those never left me, his expression one of darkest delight pursuing a tender morsel he wanted to devour.

All the nothingness I imagined...he was nothing like any of that at all.

I had grossly underestimated the man my father paid, because this man wasn't a pawn at all. Not like the others who had been sent for me over the past seven years. For the first time, I thought I might lose my bargain with myself. To fight and not die. Suddenly, those odds seemed insurmountable.

Poisoned? I gasped, drawing in quick, sharp breaths that didn't do enough to fill my lungs. A soft laugh left his lips as I studied him, and he leaned down to whisper a breath across my parched lips.

"Only for a short time. I wanted to be able to ruin you, fuck you without your screams waking the building. A little whisper of a scream is enough for me. Will you give me that?" he asked so politely, as though requesting an afternoon stroll.

My room? I mouthed, blinking rapidly at him as my lungs stalled.

His fingers brushed my forehead, and he perched

on the edge of my bed. "Breathe, Wintergreen," he murmured, stroking my cheeks. His hand pinched my chin when I didn't answer him. "Breathe," he demanded, holding my face up so I strained against the ropes at my wrists, their cruel knots softer than I expected them to be. "Slowly. If you stop breathing it will be by my hand, not because you devolved into a fucking panic attack," he snarled.

Closing my eyes I nodded, inhaling a long breath through my nose, and out. Another breath eased the tightness locking my body rigid as his grip eased and he caressed my face intimately, like a lover.

Are we not?

Our game had changed, developed into something *more* over the last week... last night. Somewhere along the line I gave up my control, or he took it. I wasn't sure which it was, and that scared me almost as much as the perfect killer resting on the side of my bed.

The mattress dipped under his weight, and he used the blade of my own stolen knife from beneath my pillow to trace patterns across my exposed decolletage.

Tears collected at the corners of my eyes, trickling along my cheeks to the corners of my mouth. I tasted the salt before he leaned forward, pressing his fingers in a surprising tender gesture to the corners of my mouth.

"So beautiful. Why do you cry? Do you fear me?" he asked, the corners of his eyes crinkling with concern.

Psycho, I mouthed, watching him, but not answering the question.

He must be a good ten years older than my nineteen, maybe a little more. His early thirties, perhaps? I had never been good at guessing ages, not when my father's associates were often long term drug users who aged prematurely.

"Probably," he agreed with a small smile, running his thumb across my bottom lip, coating the skin there with my tears. "But that's not what frightens you, is it, my Wintergreen?"

I frowned a little deeper than I would usually to get my unspoken question across to him, still concentrating on my breath. Following commands.

"A question. Why do I call you that? Because you reflect starlight in your eyes, while lighting the void. But your blade has bite, and your name suggests something softer. So, the arctic starflower was my closest analogy. My Wintergreen." Seemingly satisfied with his monologue, he probed the seam of my mouth and pushed his thumb gently inside. "Suck," he murmured idly, removing my side of the conversation in its entirety.

I shuddered at the first taste of him, my mouth moving in a familiar gesture as he observed me with hungry eyes. He didn't taste bad, of gun oil and leather, perhaps. Something sharper like citrus I thought I might have scented somewhere before.

My lips made a slightly rounder shape without my permission and I jerked back slightly, letting go of his thumb with a soft popping sound that echoed in my head like a memory, or a dream. My eyes widened as I refocused on the present and him in another question, one I didn't expect him to answer.

He laughed softly again, pushing his thumb back into my mouth, and waited until I opened for him again. I twirled my tongue around the intrusion's tip as his eyes darkened.

"It is my cock you remember in your sweet mouth, Celeste. Then I came across your scars, your tits, before you woke. I didn't want to choke you to death. What an ignominious way to die." He tilted his head to one side as I sucked his thumb rhythmically. "Dignity should be preserved in death. Is that what scares you?"

I nipped the top of his thumb, and he laughed softly.

"Dirty girl. Let's put that mouth to good use, shall we?" He rose and reached for his belt, but when I expected him to unbuckle it, he slipped a thick-handled knife from his pocket, the hilt's shape bulging just like a–

I blinked and shook my head.

His smile disappeared. "Would you prefer the real thing already?" he hissed, catching my chin in the same hard pincer grip he used before.

Heat gushed between my thighs at his rough handling, and I managed to convey a strangled mewl. *Name,* I mouthed, right before he pushed the bulbous head of the blade's handle into my mouth, whetting it with my saliva and sliding it in and out a few times.

"Dante," he murmured. "Beaufort. Your father hired me to kill you. After a month of trying, yesterday, I said no."

My father will send men. My mouth was being used and I couldn't get the words out. I clenched my thighs together, feeling the heat and slick there. *I am so broken as his obsession.*

Then his words registered, and my heart stalled, an action that had nothing to do with the way he used my mouth. He'd send assassins right fucking now, if I knew my father. Take us both out, the heir and the threat, at the best possible opportunity, when the vengeance was fresh and my attacker–my lover?–was distracted.

Or was it the other way around?

I mumbled frantically around his dildo knife as he worked it slowly in and out of my mouth, but my lips were filled with the rubber cock, my throat still swollen from whatever drug he gave me. I didn't manage to make more than a whisper of sound.

He smiled, and it seemed that was how he liked it. "I can smell you, you know. Your need. Here. May I?" he asked permission again as he slowly fucked my mouth with the knife handle, and I fell into a dual state of panic and submission, parting my legs, gurgling and sucking all at once.

"So fucking perfect. So damaged and beautiful, wearing my marks," he whispered, tracing his fingers along my neckline, over the scars I wore that he gave me when he refused to take the shot to end my life.

That choice could be stripped from us both at any moment and I was utterly helpless to do anything about it. I tried to spit out the knife, but he pushed it deeper, shaking his head in warning.

"Be a good girl, Wintergreen. Let me fuck your

lovely holes tonight, and maybe I'll take you some-where so you can see tomorrow."

The promise was almost too much, and I nodded, gurgling and whining as he laughed at me. His palms grazed over my nipples, circling them and making them stiff until my noises settled and I whimpered, resigning myself to sucking the rubber cock until he let me up.

I twisted my wrist as he watched with amuse-ment tinging his lips, but he'd tied me well. So well I couldn't free myself until I used the knife somehow, or he let me.

"Permission, Wintergreen," he repeated, his voice hardening.

I nodded, closing my eyes as tears of frustration and relief cascaded along my cheeks, dampening the pillow beneath my head. He'd let me keep that, a courtesy like everything he did. A gift I could owe my life on...or his.

Swallowing a hiccup that threatened to choke me, I followed the rhythm he set, rocking the dildo gently into and out of my mouth aided by my saliva, his fingers trailed along my stomach where he tugged up my night dress to expose my pussy.

"No panties. You wanted playtime, didn't you?"

Glad the room was dark, my cheeks headed to

blazing to the chorus of his laughter again. He traced over my waxed mound, soothing the slicked flesh there, rubbing my dampness from clit to asshole, and across the tops of my thighs. I whimpered at his ministrations, my need suddenly straining against his ropes, taking his dildo deeper, needing the release.

"What if I teased you?" he asked softly, circling my clit and my entrance but never touching either. "I could edge us both, beautiful girl. All night."

A groan ripped from my filled throat, an admission of desperation. HIs eyes lit, travelling my body with a possessive gaze I instantly craved, wanting his eyes on me and no one else.

There was something I should remember but his teasing already had me on the hardest edge where a single touch would capsize me into a sea of his making, and I didn't know if I would be able to emerge the other side unscathed.

Or if I wanted to.

He pushed the knife handle a little harder. "Relax your throat for me, Wintergreen. Then, if your lips kiss the blade, I'll slide my cock into your dripping hole, and let you come."

My moan, a distorted, strangled noise was audible as he pushed on the blade. I swallowed hard, sticking my tongue out by reflex and let him ease the rubber deeper. My throat protested, and I opened my lips wide to take the offering he presented, gliding his fingers over my slicked hole. His body arched over mine, those fathomless eyes so deep I knew I lost my soul to him already. Whatever he wanted, I would give. My tongue was the first to touch the silvered blade, then my bottom lip.

He left the dildo in my throat for a long moment, letting me suffer as the tips of his fingers entered me, my tears matching my pussy as I wept for him.

My body pulsed at the welcome intrusion, my hips arching for more as he laughed at my suffering. A shadow passed behind him, one that shouldn't have been there. The next sound to come from my throat could have saved us both, but the dildo and his drug prevented all my words.

His laugh died as he fell, a muted thump vibrating my bed as he slumped against it, darkness spreading over his hair, though he didn't fall off the mattress completely. I was left with one assassin's fingers half in my pussy, my body exposed to the new intruder's eyes, and a knife dildo jammed down my throat.

The next laugh wasn't so musical, or so welcome.

Neither was the hand on the blade that forced the dildo deeper, too deep.

All at once I realized how gentle my assassin, Dante, had been.

How his obsession prevented him from hurting me.

I thrashed in my bonds, arching up to try to shove the knife into my new attacker, but his hand on my forehead held me down.

"Your father will enjoy paying me double," he croaked, delight in his face as he reached down with his free hand and rubbed his crotch.

Long enough for me to try to spit the dildo free.

He saw, and slowly shoved it back, plugging my throat, and my source of air.

"Night night, princess. I won't see you in the daylight."

My air cut off and blackness descended, and I wondered if my new assassin would be right.

A single tear tracked my cheek. Without Dante's kindness, my death would not be dignified. I would be violated by a man I didn't know, and I'd never have Dante's hands on me again.

I cried helplessly as life flickered away from me.

CHAPTER 5

DANTE

I woke the way I passed out when her father's bastard of a henchman tried to bash my skull in. With my fingers buried in her still wet pussy, a raging hard on between my legs, I was torn between stealing her away forever or killing her.

Celeste lay on a stretcher bed with me humped over the side, both legs dangling and breathing in the sweet scene of her skin. My face smushed into her stomach with a gun pressed to the back of my head.

Within seconds of waking, the urge to rain death on the three men gathered around us fell to them instead of her. A moment of abject clarity fell over me as I recognized I never intended to kill her.

Because I fucking loved her, worshipped everything about her.

That the three men standing in the shadows watching me defile her stunning, lithe body were present left my need to claim her that much stronger. I flicked my wrist, sliding the crossbow bolt from beneath my wrist as I half-stood, leaning over her to check she breathed.

Her chest rose, and mine loosened with the motion. *Good.* That she still lived only prevented me from killing the three men now instead of later, but I needed to secure her first.

"Wintergreen," I mumbled, ignoring the gun grinding a bald patch into the back of my head. My mouth filled with what felt like sandpaper, only it was my tongue that stuck to the roof of my mouth. "Wake up, pretty girl." Not that I wanted her awake, but I needed to know she wasn't so damaged she couldn't wake.

Her breaths grew erratic as she came out of her faint, as though registering already what was happening to her, the fucking *wrongness* of it all.

And as a hired killer, this situation was all sorts of fucked up. Especially when the first rotund man stepped forward and opened his mouth.

"I see you've met my daughter." Mandillion

Flores slipped his hands into his pockets and rocked on his heels, a pleased expression creasing his face as I watched him from the corner of my eye.

He flicked his fingers at me from his pockets, indicating to the man behind me to step back. I half snorted. If I made the same motion, his daughter would come on my hand.

Celeste choked as she came around, gasping a little louder than she'd been able to when I played with her.

But the rules of this engagement changed. I wasn't certain what they were yet, but I could take a solid guess.

Risking taking my eyes off the small-time gangster who was well out of his league, I turned to her, sliding the bolt from my free hand and palming it to hers in a seamless movement.

Wake up enough to take what could save your life, you fucking beautiful little killer.

I looked her up in my off hours, not being consumed with watching the physical version of my obsession and caved to stalking her digitally instead. She had at least eight kills to her name, all the same sort: hired hits from her father or others, the youngest when she was twelve, taking the garrot the man fumbled, nimbly climbing over his bulky form that worked against him and twisting it around his neck. She was so damn small the behemoth couldn't reach her as she bit through his skin and into his esophagus.

The others followed suit until the perfect nineteen-year-old was as cold on the inside as she was outside.

"Keep your other hand where I can see it," snapped her father's man, the one with the gun.

The third remained in the shadows, unmoving, observing. I sensed the power play in motion and knew I didn't have to worry about her father, just the other two.

He would meet his just end shortly, by one of our hands.

Celeste clenched around mine, her body twisting slightly as she realized my hand was still lodged inside her, deeper than I had been before. Her soft moan sent blood evacuating from my head, but I didn't need the distraction of arousal right now, not if she was to live.

Me... I wasn't so certain about a future. Right now had to be about her.

"You may play with her. I'd like to see her have a good fuck before I end her," her father sneered. "She's been useless, playing in her little studio, making *pictures*. How fucking pathetic. A waste of money. The mafia grounds of her choice at her pickings and this is what she does with her life."

"You caged me," she whispered, her body bearing down on me again.

My little Wintergreen wanted to continue our one-sided conversation, if the roles were somewhat reversed. I was good with that.

"Tell me what you need, baby," I murmured under my breath, low enough for her to hear, but no one else. Her hand closed around the bolt, and she tucked it into her side, her eyes wide with fear while she dripped down my wrist. "Because this is turning me the fuck on and I can't spare the headspace for it." I winked, feeling the scar on my face pull.

Her hand lifted, and she reached for me, stroking the skin. "What happened?" she whispered, her brow dipping.

"I'll tell you when you earn our way outta here," I murmured, letting my French accent thicken.

Her eyes widened at the small extra bit of information. I'd learned so much about her, but she knew—or should know—almost nothing about me.

She nodded as her father hissed, his boot connecting with the base of my spine. I grimaced as pain shot up my lower back, one knee contacting the bare cement ground hard.

"Fuck her already," her father groused. "At least I let you keep your hand in her so she's a proper little puppet." He laughed, a hideous sound that echoed around the room.

My foot grazed something metal and I glanced down at the drain beneath us.

Fuck.

Shit was about to get serious.

The gun that had been at the back of my head when I awoke reappeared, digging in and forcing my face toward her cunt.

"You could lick her instead," the man sneered. "Taste the princess before you both die. A good death, yes?" His accent reminded me of home and I shuddered under the memory.

French fucking mafia.

Le Milieu.

Suddenly it hit me who the man who remained in the shadows was.

The gun bore into my head and I leaned into the motion, looking up only to hold Celeste's gaze of starlight and ice.

"I'm sorry," I murmured, working my fingers

inside her body, letting my head be shoved down and licking her clit.

Her body stiffened at the motions, and I worked her as hard as I would had we been alone. Because this part, it seemed, was necessary to buy ourselves a few more seconds. If my guess was correct, both her father–disgustingly–and the shadowed man would edge forward and take a piece of the action.

Leon Verrmilieu had been my father's second. I never bothered to listen to what happened with his arm of the French Mafia after I left the country, working my way across Europe and into the US. I hadn't much cared. But suddenly that ignorance appeared to be a really shitty life choice on my behalf.

I soothed Celeste's skin as she fought the sensations rolling through her body, working my hand fluidly inside her, curling my fingers into her flesh and teasing the spots that would draw out her orgasm longest. I kept my mouth pressed to her skin, licking around my fingers to torture her flesh from the outside.

Her stifled whimpers left my cock aching to sink into her; God alone knew what it did to the men watching the display we gave them on command like a pair of dogs in heat.

She shuddered again as I nipped her clit, her pussy pulsing as I drew her closer to bliss.

"Come for me, Celeste," I used her name, trying to get the message I needed across to her as the man behind me moved forward, reaching to squeeze her breast. "*Now*," I commanded into her skin.

I removed my fingers from her body, yanking my head back to halt her impending orgasm. She couldn't come. Not if we were going to live.

I'll make it up to you, Wintergreen. I promise. However the fuck you want. Listen to what I can't say to you.

Her hand holding the bolt shot forward and lodged itself into the man's thigh through his black slacks. Thank God for fashion conscious mafia. If he'd been wearing jeans, the ploy might never have worked. She ripped the bolt, already buried deep, to the side. There was no way the man's artery didn't split from the way warm blood splattered her breast, and the side of my face.

The man screamed obscenities, clutching her hand and half dragging her off the table before anyone else in the room could react. His drama queening as his life blood sang freely from his veins gave me the perfect cover.

Good girl, I mouthed at Celeste, red dripping

from us both as I whirled with slippery hands and scooped up the man's gun from his grip, firing off two rounds through his spread legs.

Both hit the man at the back of the room and as he fell forward I knew my assumption was correct. My father's second fell face first into a pool of his own gray matter leaking from his shattered skull. He wouldn't have killed Celeste; he would have sold her virginity–if I assumed correctly–to the next highest bidder. I wondered if her father knew that, but decided I didn't care. He wouldn't live long enough to do any more damage to her.

I fired the next shot straight up, through the man's groin above me, and into his innards.

He too fell, writhing in a spreading stain of scarlet sin, already stinking of piss and shit.

It didn't matter if he didn't die immediately; he was in too much pain and my Wintergreen's damage path shortened his life expectancy to a few dozen breaths at most.

Her father I watched and held the gun out to my side.

Celeste's fingers covered mine, and she took the weapon with hesitancy.

I cocked my head to one side, not looking at her this time, but watching her father. Noting could stop him from dying but I didn't trust the slimy asshole not to pull another gun or knife on his daughter who he was prepared to watch be raped in front of him for fuck's sake.

Even I had some morals.

Trafficking, pedophilia and incest were right the fuck up there. Right alongside animal mutilation and misuse.

Besides, Celeste was mine.

"You've done well, daughter," her father faked his pleasure, limping forward, one hand outstretched. "Now give daddy the gun, honey."

I nearly puked on the man dying at my feet.

"I've never shot anyone," she murmured.

I cocked her a half grin, still watching her father. The man stammered over a few unintelligible sentences as she raised the gun, and fell silent.

"You almost shot me, that night."

"That was a crossbow."

There's a difference?" I grinned in full. "Point, look down the barrel. Same rules. It's loaded and primed. Squeeze gently, Wintergreen. Double tap, nice and sharp."

"You fucking–"

She offloaded four rounds in quick succession.

Two in her father's shoulder, one in the chest and one in the throat.

Her father's body fell and she looked at me, her face speckled with blood. She shrugged. "I wanted to be sure."

I grinned, scooting closer to her and wrapping my arms tight around her body. "So beautiful. So perfect."

"You're going to stroke my ego."

"I'll do more than that." I climbed onto the stretcher, working my belt.

She watched me with trepidation. "Dante–"

I leaned down and kissed her hard. Our first kiss. "I know. I'll make you mine the way I always planned."

"In a room full of dead bodies?" Her eyes flicked to the doorway and I pulled the gun to her side.

"In a way you'll never say no to me again. Shoot anyone who comes through that door while I fuck you, okay?" I added casually, just to see the shock written on her face.

Celeste didn't disappoint. The wide-eyed look she gave me almost made me cover her with ropes of cum on the spot. Her lips parted on a breath and I swore to fuck she whispered *yes*.

Jesus fuck.

I breathed hard and tapped her thighs. "Open, sweet baby girl. Let me fuck you into submission now." I held her gaze, letting mine harden.

My Wintergreen nodded, sliding her legs open for me as she had in her bed, and dropped her head back.

A deep growl built in my throat as I arched my body over hers, freeing my granite cock into my hand.

Mine.

Perfection.

CHAPTER 6

CELESTE

Dante traced his fingers along the insides of my thighs, his heavy cock hanging between us. He read the situation right; thanks to a constant turnover of my father's guards and the cages he put me in daily, I not only had no friends, I'd also never had a boyfriend. Only killers to kill in return and a father to despise.

And now my paternal gene pool lay dead, and one of his many fears for me was about to come true.

Dante ached over me, breathing hard as I gave him my surrender. I never wanted anything–or anyone–so much in my life.

Not since he sprayed shards of glass into my

chest. Or since I woke with his scent wrapped around me.

Dante played with my pussy, his fingers gentle as I submitted to whatever he wanted, relinquishing that long held control to another for the first time in full. He could have made me come, to replace the ruined orgasm he'd already given me, but he didn't need to. My body was soaked in sweat and slick with need for him.

"Please," I whispered, begging for the first time, liking how it tasted on my tongue.

Dante stilled. A deep sound ripped from his chest not dissimilar to a roar as he lunged forward, all gentle touches forgotten as he notched himself at my entrance and slammed deep inside me.

"*MINE*," he growled above me, cupping my head in his larger hand, and holding me to his chest.

I barely heard him, white hot pain obliterating everything. The pain went on and on, melding from something hard and stretched and *deep* to something bright. A scream built but was halted when the hand at the back of my head closed around my throat, throttling my breath.

"Come for me, Wintergreen. Come on my cock, you beautiful fucking creature."

I shattered, inside first around the steel rod

intrusion between my legs taking up every inch of space within me, then outside. The explosion where he rubbed my clit furiously edged on painful, obliterating the other softer pain that grew faint, a mere memory, and replacing it with a newer one.

My scream formed on my lips in the shape of his name and he kissed me again, releasing my throat and replacing my air with his.

I moaned my pleasure into his mouth, and he stole that too, dominating the kiss with hard thrusts of his tongue, pushing my mouth wider until I cried out. His hips moved in tandem until it felt like being fucked in two places at once. The sensations, all of him, was consuming. I screamed again, and he folded his large fingers around my throat, taking that sound away from me too. His presence overwhelmed me as he fucked me brutally, the cot I woke in straining beneath us.

Pleasure worked its way from my toes to my spine and travelled upward in an unbearable shiver. I bit into his shoulder, tasting his blood as he pounded me. The bed wobbled and collapsed, taking us both to the floor. His arms wound tight around me, crushing me to him and softening the fall that only jarred him deeper inside me.

But Dante never stopped fucking me so hard I

was certain my insides would be rubbed raw. Bliss obliterated the present until he roared in my ear, coming hard enough to jerk his body deeper than ever. His release filled me, plugged inside by his cock as he sealed us together in a tangle of pleasure and pain.

"You're mine, forever. Do you understand that?" he rasped, catching my face in his hands. "Tell me you do, Wintergreen, or I'll keep fucking you until you agree to it."

I laughed, a sound that turned to a half sob as tears ran down my face. "Why am I crying?" I whispered in a shaky voice that sounded nothing like mine.

"Because you are a beautiful, sweet creature forced into a life too hard for who you are." His hand pressed over my heart that throbbed for him.

I frowned, my pussy aching as he moved like he might rise. I slammed my hands on his ass, desperate to keep him inside me, filled. "Don't you dare move. Wait. How do you know who I am?"

He braced his forearms above my head, looking down at me with the sort of possession I dreamed about in my worst nightmares. The inescapable sort, because not only would this man kill for me, he would kill me if he felt he had to. My legs trembled as I shook around him.

"Because I watched you. You've strained against this cage your father built for you, a shitty prison designed for a mafia princess, but you, my beautiful creature, are just a princess, forced into a mafia life. I know what happens to women like you. They turn into people like my mother, twisted and damaged and so motherfucking wrong. I won't let that happen to you, Wintergreen."

I blinked at him. "Okay."

He smiled and it lit his face, even the sliced, scarred side. "Okay?"

I let the tears fall, but no longer sobbed. "Am I trading one cage for another?"

He frowned. "What do you want you didn't have? Freedom? It's yours. Walk from me now, if you want. But believe me when I tell you you'll never be alone, and I'll kill anyone who touches you."

Something dark and hot built in my chest. "And if I stay?"

He held me fiercely to his chest, rocking us both as he peppered my face with kisses. "You'll want for nothing and no one will ever treat you wrong or hurt you." He paused and thought for a moment. "Except maybe me."

I hiccup-giggled, all the emotions blowing out of me at once. "My art?"

"Make whatever you like," he promised me, finding my mouth in a deep, hard kiss I felt to my core. I pulsed around him as his cock hardened inside me again. "But I get to take what I like too, you understand me?" He rocked his hips forward, his possessive hold claiming me even as I claimed him. "Even if you're sore, you take me, and I'll reward you with all the pleasure you can handle."

"And...lo–" I closed my eyes, more tears leaking out.

I couldn't say the word, let alone feel it. Could I? My father had been an absent parent, and I never knew my mother. He killed her when I was a baby for not yielding sons. A wonderful upbringing. I didn't know love.

His hands framed my face as he began to move slowly within me, careful of my tender body, stretching me as he thickened impossibly until my sobs and moans and hiccups merged into a cacophony of wanton sound.

"You don't know I love you? For the weeks I watched you, when I intended to end your life... beautiful girl. I saw so much in you to adore, to free. But only if you're mine," he whispered.

It took my mind a few moments to catch up. "You...love me?" I whispered brokenly.

A small pulse of pleasure tore over me, obliterating my vision of him. When my sight cleared, still sparking at the edges, I trembled in his arms as he smiled down at me tenderly.

"I love you," he murmured. "I'll kill for you, care for you. Until the day you don't want me."

"And then you'll stalk me," I giggled, high on a heady dose of euphoria.

"Then I'll stalk you," he agreed.

"What if I can't say the same back?"

His face darkened. "You don't know how it feels?"

I shrugged. "I've never had anyone love me, or know how to love." Not so much as a pet.

He kissed me as slow as he fucked me, long, languorous strokes of his tongue gliding along mine. "Would you kill me if I gave you a knife or a gun now?"

I stared at him and shook my head. Pressure built in my throat and I tried to swallow past it but couldn't. "No," I forced out.

He nodded thoughtfully, rocking us gently amidst the catastrophe of bodies and broken bedding. "Your heart, would it hurt if I walked away from you right now?" He leaned back, his arms loosening as though he would withdraw, his face closed.

My chest clamped down, and my breath stalled. "No!" I gasped. I locked my legs around his waist. "Don't- don't–" I shouldn't have asked him. I should have just gone with whatever he said–

Dante sank deep into me, tightening his hold until there wasn't a breath between us anywhere. "That is love, Wintergreen. Where parting makes you want to scream, and giving warms you. Loss feels like an eternal void that can't be bridged. When all you want is to be with that person forever." He nuzzled my neck, nipping and licking his hurts. "It might take some time to recognize it. Build on it. I know you've–"

"I love you," I blurted.

The pressure in my chest eased, replaced with a heat consuming me from the inside.

He blinked. "Don't rush this, Celeste. I won't let you take those words back."

"I'm not taking them back," I whispered. "And I'm not letting you let me go either. But if you don't fuck me properly again, I might hurt you. I still have a gun," I added, just to spice up the bargain. I waved the weapon off to one side, my finger over the trigger but holding it carefully aimed away, toward the body of my father.

What? The asshole could come back.

Dante laughed, surprise lighting his face for a split second before he slammed his hand over the wrist holding the gun, slapping my hand into the cement floor. His other hand gripped my hip, digging in hard enough to mark as he let loose his rage and fucked me like I was the only obsession he every harbored, or ever wanted.

His kisses softened, and he growled down at me once more before he stole my breath again.

Mine, he mouthed.

Then neither of us had breath to speak with for a long, long time.

CHAPTER 7

DANTE

I woke in my house in the mountains overlooking the college lands from a distance with Celeste on my chest. Her breaths were soft, her scars smooth beneath my fingers as I traced over them. We collected the few things we needed from her old apartment, set off the fire alarm to evacuate it and burned the place to the ground. It turned out her father owned the entire building, and ran an illegal brothel from its rooms with often undocumented girls and minors as his 'hosts'.

With the man dead and my father's second I learned took over his territory and was now negotiating to take over Celeste's father's reign behind his back still oozing brains in the basement of the building where we shot them all, she was safe. The territory would be taken out by others, but Celeste had never been an active part of her father's networking, and her sheltered life worked in our favor.

The local gangs met over a barrel of the Frenchman's rare cognac, quaffing it like the cheap shit they probably thought it was and divvied up the land like it was so many properties on a board game.

I held Celeste to me throughout that meeting, each of us holding a loaded gun, though thankfully neither of us had to use them. The deal was simple. Work out the lands they wanted, and we walked away.

Her bank account remained hers, though with the fund I earned myself over the years as a hired killer, neither of us had to do anything we didn't want for the rest of our lives. Celeste opted to remain studying at Rippton U, and I would take her down the mountain on my bike each day for classes once the semester resumed after the holidays.

Right now we had a few days of peace, and time to discover each other the right way instead of sneaking glances and watching from the shadows.

My heart held enough of those but Celeste was hellbent on healing me with kisses and sweet words and her own strange brand of darkness. Though waking with her head on my chest, stroking over the marks I left on her...this life couldn't get much better.

Except for maybe one thing.

I stroked her hair, loathe to wake her but my patience frayed for once. "Wake up, Wintergreen."

She mumbled something into my skin, a small patch of drool forming beneath her mouth. I laughed at the simple evidence of her humanity as she unfolded around me like a flower blooming.

"What was that?" I stroked her pale hair back from her face, tracing her stunning lips. I never did play out that fantasy of her sucking me off while she slept; it was one to keep in reserve for a rainy day, perhaps.

"Perhaps," she murmured back, blinking at me, her eyes wide. "Wait–"

"Another day," I muttered, dropping a quick kiss on her lips that spread in a wide smile I felt to the tip of my cock.

"Can another day be now?" she asked playfully, running her fingertips along my ribs.

Outside the mountain lodge I built years ago, snow drifted around us. It didn't fall as heavily here as it did in the higher peaks, but the

Christmas morning air was cold enough to leave a fire running through the night, the ember's residual glow letting us both sleep naked and wrapped around each other. Fortunately, the location meant the house was remote enough to not worry about prying neighbors while we played the twisted games I didn't think would ever stop between us.

Or maybe she was just a twisted beautiful little fuck like me, and our games would change over time. Either way, I wouldn't let her go.

"Don't you go back to sleep." I pinched her ass for the pure joy of seeing her shriek.

Her hand closed around my cock through the sheets and squeezed–really fucking hard.

"Never do that again," she threatened, jerking me dryly through the soft cotton that felt anything but in her torturous hold.

I raised my hands, slipping the object in my left palm to the back. "I surrender."

Her grip loosened and she stroked me gently. "Good boy," she purred, her eyes lit with dark fire.

My cock stood up for her, and I let her play, my precum marring the sheets with a translucent spot. "Gonna make me come without getting off? That's a nice Christmas present," I taunted her sweetly.

"Maybe," she looked at me through her lashes. "I wouldn't mind–"

That's as far as I let her get before I flipped us, slamming her onto her back with enough force to expel her breath.

"Dante," she whispered, gasping.

"Celeste," I taunted, sweeping my tongue across her mouth and ripping the blanket from between us. "Open your legs."

Wincing a little from our rough love making the night before–I held her over a wooden chair and fucked her raw from behind–she obeyed my command.

"Be gentle with me?" she begged, though lust darkened the starlight in her eyes.

"Hmm. Should I?" I asked, gripping her hand and forcing the firm band over her knuckle on her ring finger. I sized the thing when she wasn't paying attention to me while she drew one night and it wouldn't easily come off. "Or are you asking the wrong questions?"

She frowned at me, then at her hand where a black tungsten wedding band circled her finger set all the way around with tanzanite.

The color of the sky the night she threw a crossbow bolt at me.

"What is this?"

"Normally, I think I'm supposed to ask, but we're far from normal." I caught the back of her neck and bruised her lips with a hard kiss. "You're marrying me. Merry Christmas, Wintergreen."

She gasped as I broke the kiss roughly, watching her eyes. Maybe I read the whole situation wrong, but I didn't think so. She'd been abused, locked out of the world and suddenly having the world open to her–it was all too much. I tried to give her a huge room downstairs as a personal studio for her, but she ran from me, sobbing and shaking, unable to accept the gift.

And that was when I knew I couldn't give her anything more. I had to demand control from her, but I also had to be certain what I was doing was what she wanted.

Which made this moment right here really fucking important.

She swallowed as tears welled and my heart dropped.

"Celeste?" I murmured, dipping my head to kiss her a little slower.

Hovering my body above hers in the most painful plank in history became my secondary focus because all I wanted was to sink my cock into her sweet body and fuck us both to oblivion and back for the rest of the fucking holidays.

'We're getting married?" she asked, almost dreamlike as she turned the band around her fingers.

Fuck. I'd seen that look on her face before, when I was throat fucking her with the dildo knife and pinning her to her bed with my hands. Her submissive side was checking her out and I needed her consent now more than ever.

I wasn't a complete asshole, after all.

"Talk to me," I ordered, my tone hard.

She blinked fast and was back with me.

Thank fuck.

Her hand cracked across my cheek, grazing my scar that she fingered afterward when I didn't move. I never would, no matter what she hurled at me. If she needed to hit me to regain control, so be it.

We'd done worse and probably always would. Questionable morals abounded, the sort that would terrify a regular person. But that wasn't who we were.

"I'm marrying you," she sighed, sinking back into the pillows and smiling up at me. "Okay."

"Okay?" I double checked, fisting her hair and

lifting her face to mine. *Sweet Jesus, I need to taste her again. Every damn day.*

"Okay. What do you want to do?"

"Fuck you until you can't breathe," I muttered, swiping a hand over my face. *Fuck.* I hadn't fucked her up that bad. She still had free will. Mostly.

Her cute as hell giggle left me throbbing and I didn't bother holding back any longer, sinking into her hot, sopping body already soaked with my cum to fill her again and again.

"I meant for a wedding," she breathed.

"You can kill as many people as you like," I said automatically.

She moaned as I sank deeper, her blunt nails digging into my shoulder blades. "I want to wear a white silk dress. Like the one I ruined. But I want you to ruin it," she whispered.

I choked and nearly came on the spot while she dissolved into more of those delicious giggles around me. I'd fuck her until she screamed for that. Just, I needed to catch my breath first. Because this girl. My Wintergreen.

She was mine. Forever. On the best day of the year because...

I swore I'd never get sick of saying it.

Merry fucking Christmas to me.

EPILOGUE

DANTE

I slipped my cock across Celeste's lips as she slept, just enough to part them. I waited for hours, making sure she was deep asleep, refusing to fuck her all night. She whined and begged so fucking prettily, but I wanted a heavy load to fill her pretty mouth with, wanted to watch her choke on my cum as she woke, swallowing me with a little outside help.

After all, I'd help her and make sure she didn't really get hurt, seeing as this was a fantasy we both seemed to share. It hasn't escaped me at Christmas the way her stomach muscles clenched as she nearly came on the spot when I mentioned the scene as she woke, her pretty lips parting then in the fading memory of how I plugged her moans with my cock the first night I was in her room.

And after four weeks of waiting and teasing, mentioning it while my fingers were embedded deep inside her, knowing she clenched on me, I finally made that fantasy come true.

Reaching down, I thumbed her nipples through her silk nightie–white, of course, why break a good habit? She had a whole cupboard of the things, enough that I could ruin them as often as I liked, or when she craved my brand of violence on nights when her thoughts turned too dark and a good fuck wasn't enough to bring her back.

Teasing her today did it for me, and I was ready to blow as I placed my cock at her mouth, rolling her nipples through the silk. She seemed to like that, the extra slippery layer, I learned, tasting her until her need filled the bedroom with her heady scent.

Her first moan was so beautiful I couldn't break it, swiping beads of precum along her bottom lip instead as I gently caressed her.

She moaned again, her tongue slipping out to catch the moisture and I couldn't hold back any longer. I pushed my cock into her mouth, rocking my hips gently as I pumped, encouraging her to open. We'd had plenty of deep throating practice, and she relaxed nicely for me as I pushed inside, her lips closing naturally around my shaft, sucking sweetly.

"Jesus fuck," I managed, my balls drawing up tight in seconds from the perfect pressure she provided.

I reached back, playing with her pussy where she dripped obscenely on my sheets. Three fingers dove straight in and she lurched on the bed, her eyelids fluttering as she woke. Her throat flexed around my length, fight coming into her motions, but I refused to stop playing with her hot little pussy. She came on my fingers, once then again.

When I was done, releasing her body to clasp her head in both hands, I held her to my root as I came straight down her relaxed throat. She shuddered, swallowing and gagging alternately by reflex, but she had nowhere to push as I kept my cock lodged in her mouth. Her tongue flicked at my head and I groaned aloud at the sight of her waking fully around my length while I came inside her mouth.

Tears poured from her eyes as she stared up at me, bewildered and swallowing. I shouted her name to the mountains, digging my fingers into her scalp, trying to stay sane enough to ensure she didn't actually choke on me.

Her palms pressed gently against my bare thighs, but she didn't dig them in or force me back, trying her best to accommodate my size.

"So fucking beautiful," I murmured, backing off far enough that she could breathe.

Her tongue stroked my length as she sucked me gently, cleaning me, humming with me in her mouth. Shivers wracked my body, the sensations almost too great. I pushed back but she shook her head, her lips locked around me as she continued to work my length, until I hardened again.

"You wanna go again, Wintergreen?" I murmured, stroking her hair lovingly.

She nodded, tilting her head back and offering me her throat.

I groaned, gripping her shoulders and throwing her against the edge of the bed so her head hung off the end. One hand gripping her throat, I straddled her mouth, sinking in until I could feel her breaths from her nose against the sensitive skin on my balls.

Then I pushed deeper, sawing in and out of her mouth with my hand closed around her throat to feel each time my length cut off her air, and how far down I managed to go.

When she writhed, I leaned down, sucking her nipples then closed my mouth around her pussy, nipping and licking as she swallowed around me.

This time when I nutted in her mouth I didn't go alone. Her muffled cries would be a memory I could jerk off to whenever she wasn't with me. And when she was...well.

Maybe we'd set a new benchmark. I couldn't wait to set more.

Thank you for reading Dante and Celeste's story! I hope you enjoyed this wander into the darker side of romance. Please do leave a review. I love knowing what you thought of the story!!

Rippton U has its own multi world series. Start with OFF BOARDING, and watch out for Beau, who has a few things in common with Dante.